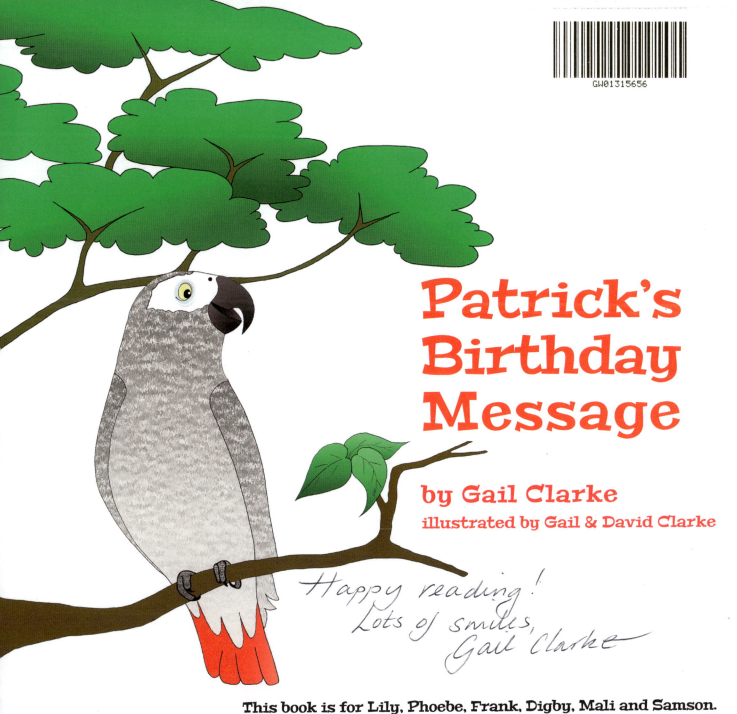

Patrick's Birthday Message

by Gail Clarke

illustrated by Gail & David Clarke

*Happy reading!
Lots of smiles,
Gail Clarke*

This book is for Lily, Phoebe, Frank, Digby, Mali and Samson.

And, of course, it's for ....Lucas........ (your name)

Patrick the parrot – an African Grey –
Was remarkably clever in every way.
With a cherry-red tail and a shiny black beak,
He had beauty and brains and what's more he could speak
The language of humans, of animals too;
There was simply no end to the things he could do!

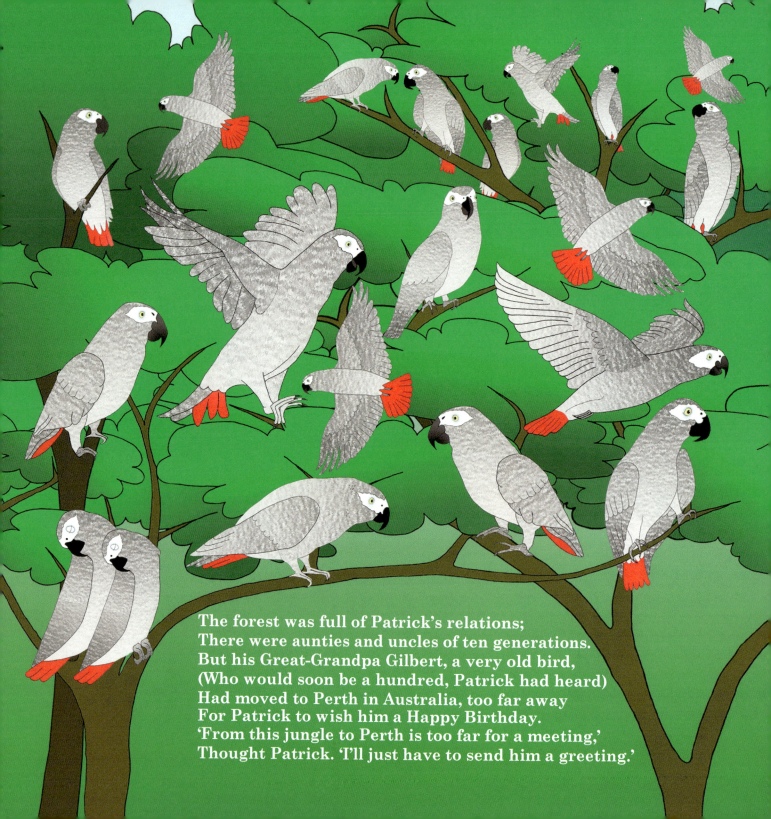

The forest was full of Patrick's relations;
There were aunties and uncles of ten generations.
But his Great-Grandpa Gilbert, a very old bird,
(Who would soon be a hundred, Patrick had heard)
Had moved to Perth in Australia, too far away
For Patrick to wish him a Happy Birthday.
'From this jungle to Perth is too far for a meeting,'
Thought Patrick. 'I'll just have to send him a greeting.'

The idea was a good one, but oh dearie me!
There was just one big problem that Patrick could see:
A round-the-world message – how could he do it?
There must be an answer if only he knew it.
An email, a letter or even a card
Was out of the question – it was simply too hard.

Then out of the blue a way became clear.
"Hip hooray!" Patrick squawked, in one joyful cheer.
He remembered a tale he had heard long ago
About swallows who hated the cold and the snow.

When winter arrived in the north they would fly
For thousands of miles every day through the sky
To South Africa's Cape, where they'd settle and stay,
Till summer at home called them back the same way.

'A swallow could carry a message part-way
To wish my great-grandpa a happy birthday!'

But when would the swallows be passing them by?
This question now needed a hasty reply.
Patrick talked to his aunt who was clever and wise
And the answer she gave was a happy surprise.
"If my memory's correct, I'd be willing to say
That the first flock of swallows arrives here today."
"Thank you, dear aunt – I must go, I can't wait
To stay for a chat or I might be too late!"

Patrick waited all day and into the night,
Hoping the swallows would pause in their flight.
He tried not to doze, though his shoulders were stooping,
His body was tired and his feathers were drooping.
Then a sound like a distant beating or humming
Made him sit up and listen – from where was it coming?

Patrick looked up and through one sleepy eye
Saw a black swirling cloud in the darkening sky.
It suddenly paused and turned slowly around,
Then it broke up and fell – like rain to the ground.
"The swallows are here, my auntie was right;
There are more than a thousand!" he squawked in delight.

But they all looked so tired and in need of a rest;
Patrick knew he should wait to make his request.
'Tomorrow will do,' he thought with a yawn,
'Tomorrow I'll ask; I'll be up with the dawn.'

And true to his word he awoke at first light
And looking around saw a wonderful sight.
Their heads were red-brown, their chins and throats too,
Their beaks and feet black, their feathers royal blue.
Their breasts were much paler, Patrick could see,
And their forked tails, like streamers, fanned out in a V.

"Excuse me," said Patrick, in a squawk most polite,
"I know you are busy preparing for flight."

"What is it, young parrot, that you'd like to know?
You'll have to be quick as we really must go."

Patrick wasted no time and in words loud and clear
He told all the swallows about his idea.
"We think," they replied, "it's an excellent plan!
We'll carry your message as far as we can.
The Cape's where we're going, you probably know,
And farther than that we simply can't go.
But a dolphin or whale, we are sure we can say,
Will carry your message the rest of the way."

And with that they flew off, rising into the sky.
Patrick waved to them all, squawking loudly, "Goodbye!"

The journey was long; they thought they would fry
In the scorching hot sun of the African sky.

And then there were storms which tossed them around,
The rain pelted down and they feared they'd be drowned.

But at last they arrived – the Cape was in sight –
The swallows had ended their marathon flight!

Several days later, when rested and strong,
It was time to pass Patrick's message along.
So a small group of swallows kept watch from a height
To see if the whales were somewhere in sight.

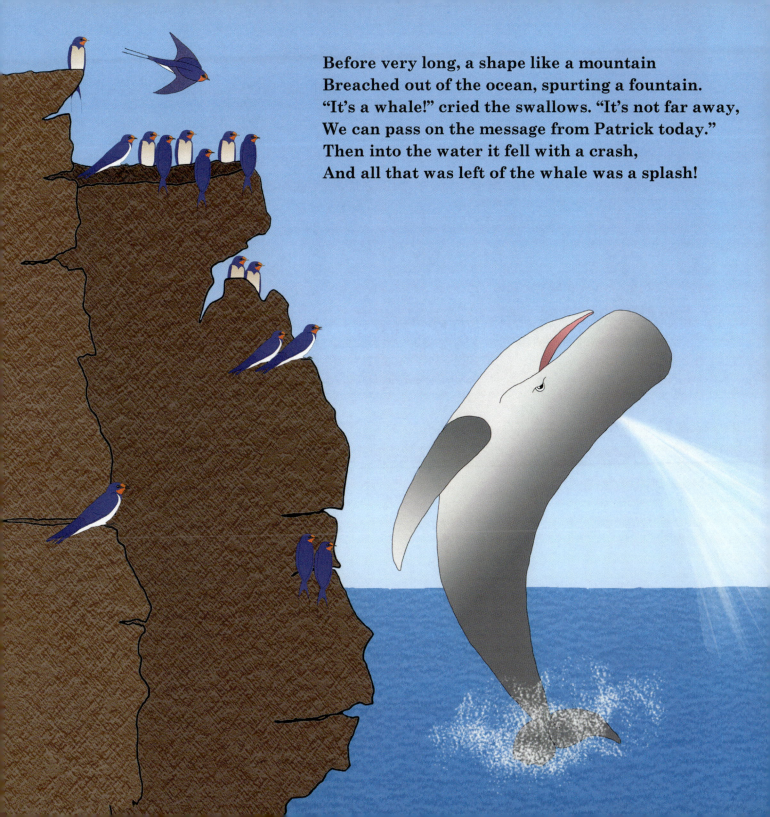

Before very long, a shape like a mountain
Breached out of the ocean, spurting a fountain.
"It's a whale!" cried the swallows. "It's not far away,
We can pass on the message from Patrick today."
Then into the water it fell with a crash,
And all that was left of the whale was a splash!

The swallows swooped down as again the whale rose
To breathe through his blowhole (a kind of whale nose).
As they circled around him, each opened his throat
And the message was sung to the whale, note by note.

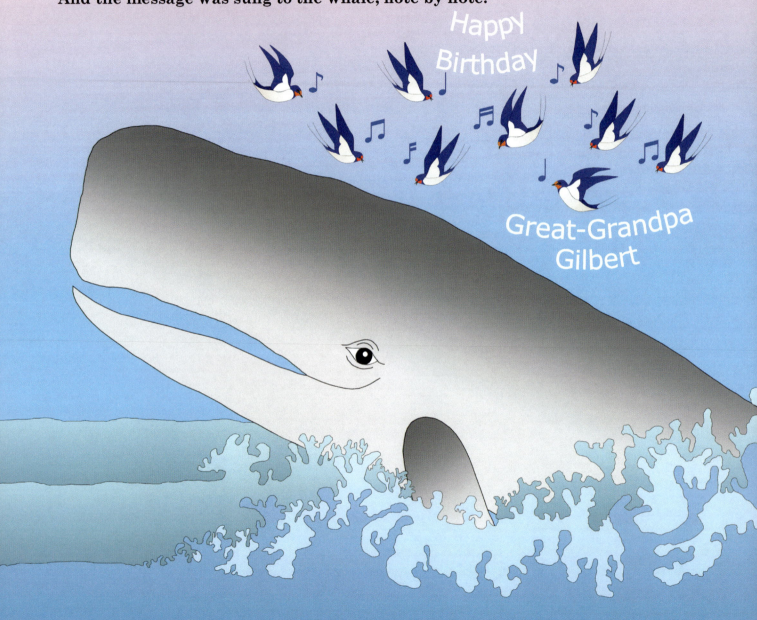

And as he dived back to the ocean's dark floor
The whale echoed the song in a deep, haunting roar.

♪ Happy Birthday ♫
Great Grandpa Gilbert

From whale to whale in continuing motion
The greeting was passed through the Indian Ocean.
And last with the message of more than a dozen
Was a bottlenose dolphin (the whales' distant cousin)
Who entered the harbour where Great-Grandpa G
Snoozed on a branch of a coolabah tree.

The dolphin sang out in notes loud and clear
Which found their way straight to Great-Grandpa's ear!

Gilbert jumped up and down, looped the loop in mid-flight,
"A greeting from Patrick!" he squawked in delight.
"Thanks, Mr. Dolphin, for bringing to me
This message that's travelled by air and by sea."

The dolphin smiled back, then called out, "By the way,
Have a great party on your special day!"
"I will," replied Gilbert, "I'm off now to bake
A huge and delicious parrot-seed cake!"

Parrot Quiz

Have a go at Patrick's quiz and see how many answers you know.

Remember, Patrick is a very clever parrot and quite tricky too, so there may be more than one correct answer for some of the questions!

Migration means:

[ ] moving from England to Africa   [ ] going to Australia

[ ] going on holiday   [ ] moving from one area or country to another

Birds migrate because:

[ ] they want to make new friends   [ ] they like holidays

[ ] they want a safe place to lay eggs and rear their young

[ ] they want to find a warmer climate

African grey parrots are:

[ ] all the colours of the rainbow   [ ] green and yellow

[ ] mostly grey with red tail feathers

African grey parrots:

[ ] always live to be a hundred years old

[ ] never live to be a hundred years old

[ ] can live to be a hundred years old

In the winter swallows fly:

[ ] north [ ] west [ ] south [ ] east

Swallows have:

[ ] blue wings, red brown throats and paler bodies

[ ] yellow beaks ad black heads [ ] grey bodies and brown tails

Swallows' tails are:

[ ] shaped like a fan [ ] V-shaped [ ] very short and pointed

Whales breathe:

[ ] through water like fish [ ] through their blowholes

[ ] they don't need to breathe

Whales:

[ ] can talk to birds [ ] cannot communicate

[ ] can communicate with each other by making underwater noises

Good Luck!
You can find the answers on my website:
www.gailclarkeauthor.com

Parrot Points

African grey parrots are among the most intelligent of all birds.

Parrots are excellent climbers because their first and fourth toes are turned backwards.

Thousands of parrots are taken from the wild illegally each year. Only parrots that have been bred in captivity should be kept as pets.

While there are over 350 species of parrots of different shapes and colours, all parrots have curved beaks perfect for cracking into seeds and nuts.

In Chinese art, parrots are considered symbols of freedom and opportunity.

From the Author

Dear Readers,

When I was writing this story I discovered lots of interesting facts about animals and migration. Did you know that some animals travel thousands of kilometres every year?

Can you find out about other animals which migrate? I have two other stories about animal migration that are pictured below ('Cosmos' and 'Skye'). You can find out more about them and my other books on my website.

If you want to ask any questions about this story or the others, or tell me something interesting about migrating animals, I should love to hear from you.

gail@gailclarkeauthor.com
www.gailclarkeauthor.com

Other Illustrated Children's Books by Gail Clarke

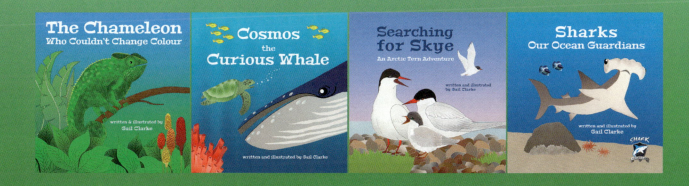

Copyright © 2013 Gail Clarke
All rights reserved
ISBN-13: 9781494896539
ISBN-10: 1494896532
www.gailclarkeauthor.com

Made in the USA
Charleston, SC
22 September 2014